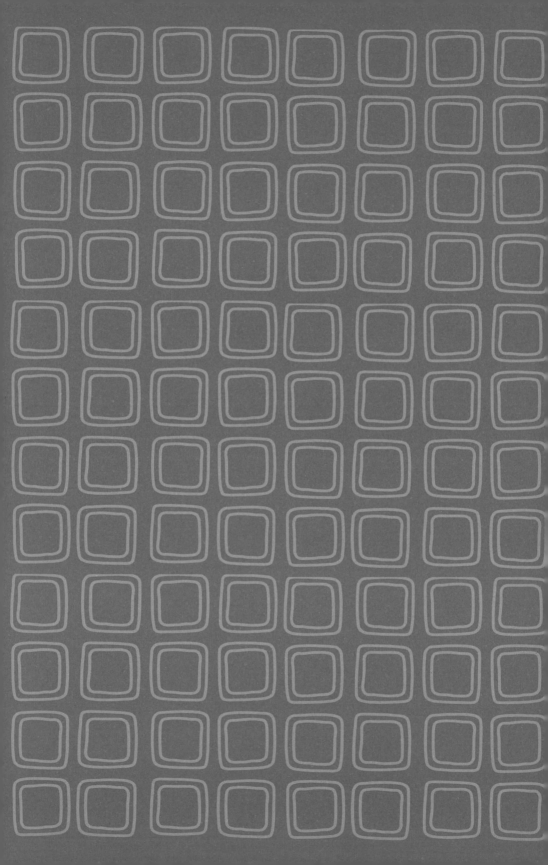

LEAF it to DOT

LEAF It to DOT

CANDLEWICK
ENTERTAINMENT

Jim Henson
THE JIM HENSON COMPANY

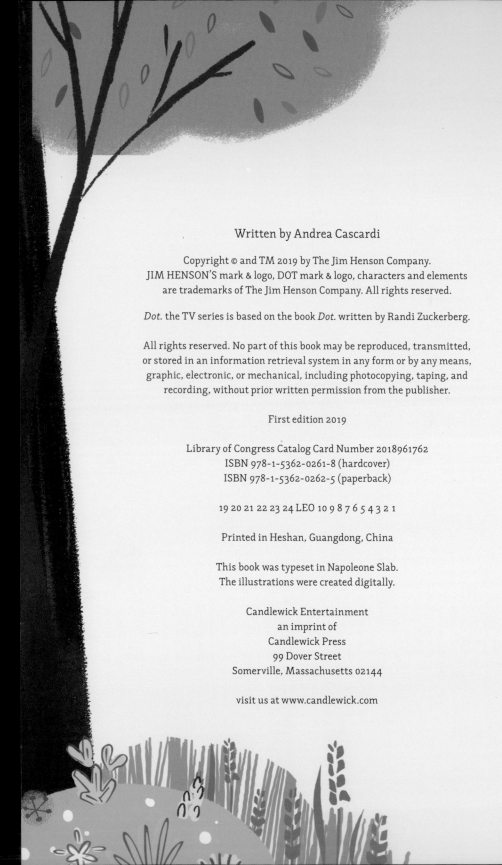

Written by Andrea Cascardi

First edition 2019

Library of Congress Catalog Card Number 2018961762
ISBN 978-1-5362-0261-8 (hardcover)
ISBN 978-1-5362-0262-5 (paperback)

19 20 21 22 23 24 LEO 10 9 8 7 6 5 4 3 2 1

Printed in Heshan, Guangdong, China

This book was typeset in Napoleone Slab.
The illustrations were created digitally.

Candlewick Entertainment
an imprint of
Candlewick Press
99 Dover Street
Somerville, Massachusetts 02144

visit us at www.candlewick.com

Contents

Chapter 1

RANGEROO SCAVENGER HUNT

Dot, Hal, Dad, and Scratch were on a Rangeroo Scavenger Hunt.

"I can't wait to get my badge!" said Hal.

"I loved being a Rangeroo," said Dad. "It's great to be out here with nothing but the trees, the birds, and the fresh air."

Dot took out her tablet.

"How can you earn your scavenger hunt badge with your eyes on a screen?" Dad asked.

"We need it to earn the badge," Dot said.

She tapped her tablet. The Rangeroo leader appeared. "Coo coo coo, Rangeroos. Are you ready to start your scavenger hunt?"

"We're ready!" said Dot and Hal.

"Use your Rangeroo scrapbook app to take pictures. Look for a beetle, animal tracks, a bird of prey, and a flowering tree. When you have found them all, you will get your scavenger hunt badges," she said.

Dot and Hal looked at the screen.

Dad looked up at the sky. "Look, a great horned owl!" he said. "It's a bird of prey!"

"A what? Where?" said Dot and Hal.

"You missed it while you were looking at the screen! The best tools for scavenger hunting are your own two eyeballs. Let an old-fashioned Rangeroo show you how it's done," said Dad.

Dad made owl noises. Dot used her
tablet to make some, too. "Hoot!"

"I hear an owl!" Dad said.

"That was the app," Dot said. "It can do other sounds, too."

She looked at her tablet.

Dad looked at the ground. He saw a hoofprint!

"Missing something?" asked Dad. "Under your noses?"

Dot moved the tablet. "Animal tracks!"

"Exactly. Guess what animal they're from," Dad said.

Dot took a picture with her tablet.

The Rangeroo leader popped up from the screen.

"Coo coo coo, Rangeroos! You found moose tracks!

"That leaves three more things to find. Go, Rangeroos, go go go!" said the Rangeroo leader. Then she was gone.

Chapter 2

TO APP OR NOT TO APP?

"How did that app know we found moose tracks?" asked Dad.

Dot showed Dad how it worked. "The app compares our photo to others until it finds a match."

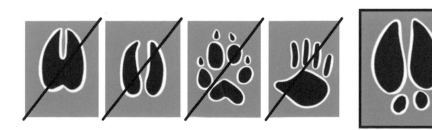

"Not bad. But I think it was more fun when you followed the tracks to find out what made them," said Dad. "I was a brave Rangeroo tracking an unknown wild beast. I pushed away a branch and there he was: the biggest moose in the forest! Old Majestic."

Hal showed Dad a photo of a moose on Dot's tablet.

"Cute. But it's no Old Majestic," said Dad.

Scratch barked and ran to a log. Hal spotted a beetle crawling on it. "That's the most amazing bug I've ever seen!" he said.

"And a beetle is on our scavenger hunt list," said Dot. "Good work!"

"Fun fact," said Dad. "This bug isn't just any beetle. It's actually a—"

Suddenly, the Rangeroo leader popped up again.

"Coo coo coo, Rangeroos! You found a beetle!

"Just two more items to find. Go, Rangeroos, go go go!" said the Rangeroo leader.

"I'm going to look up this beetle," said Dot. "It's called a scarab* beetle. They have wings hiding under their shells that they open and fly with," she read.

Dot looked up from the screen. "Where did it go?"

"It flew away," said Dad.

"And I missed it?" said Dot.

*pronounced: *SCARE-rub*

Chapter 3

CLIMB A TREE

"Hal! Look at that tree. I think it's calling us to climb it," Dot said.

Dot, Hal, and Scratch raced to the tree. Dot and Hal climbed the low branches.

"Hey, Dad. Are these flowers?" asked Dot.

"Looks like it," said Dad.

"Then this is a flowering tree," said Dot.

"And it's on our scavenger hunt list!" said Hal.

"Take a picture!" said Dot.

Dad took a picture.

The Rangeroo leader appeared again.

"Coo coo coo, Rangeroos! You found a flowering tree!"

"Yeah, but what kind of tree?" asked Dad.

"A dogwood," said the Rangeroo leader. "Only one item left to find. Go, Rangeroos, go go go!"

Dad looked at the tablet. "Not bad. Let's see what else you've got, app."

Dad took pictures as he walked.

"You found a showy mountain ash tree," the app said. "You found a trembling* aspen tree."

"You got those right. But here's one you won't know," Dad said.

"You found a goosefoot** maple tree," said the app.

"Yup, you got it," said Dad.

*pronounced: *TREM-bling*
**pronounced: *GOOS-foot*

Dot and Hal
walked ahead.
"Hoot!"
"The owl! The
bird of prey is the last
thing on our list," Dot said.

"Dad!" Dot called quietly.

Dad was busy looking at the tablet and was not looking where he was going. He took a picture.

"You have found poison ivy," said the app.

"Oh, no!" said Dad.

He gave Dot the tablet.

"I'm done," he said.

Hal looked at the great horned owl. Dot took the last picture.

"We're done, too!" said Dot.

Chapter 4
OLD MAJESTIC

The Rangeroo leader appeared.

"Coo coo coo, Rangeroos! You found a great horned owl! You've earned your scavenger hunt badges," she said.

"We did it!" said Dot and Hal.

"They'll be awarded at the next
Rangeroo meeting. Until then . . ."

Everyone chanted:

"I'm a Rangeroo, and you're one, too.

Let's say hello with a coo coo coo!

We're always helpful, don't you know.

Go, Rangeroos, go go go!"

"I've got to admit, Dot, that tablet can do some incredible stuff," Dad said.

"Yep. But old-fashioned hunting with nothing but your eyeballs is pretty cool, too," said Dot.

Scratch barked.

Looking over a bush they saw . . .
the biggest moose in the forest!

"Old Majestic!" said Dad.

"Well, hello, old friend."

36

"Our scavenger hunt was so fun. And I got my badge! My dad helped. We're going to do more hiking. There are so many things to see! Like owls, flowers, Old Majestics . . . Hey! Is that a woodpecker out there?"

"Time for me to unplug. This is Dot, signing off for now!"

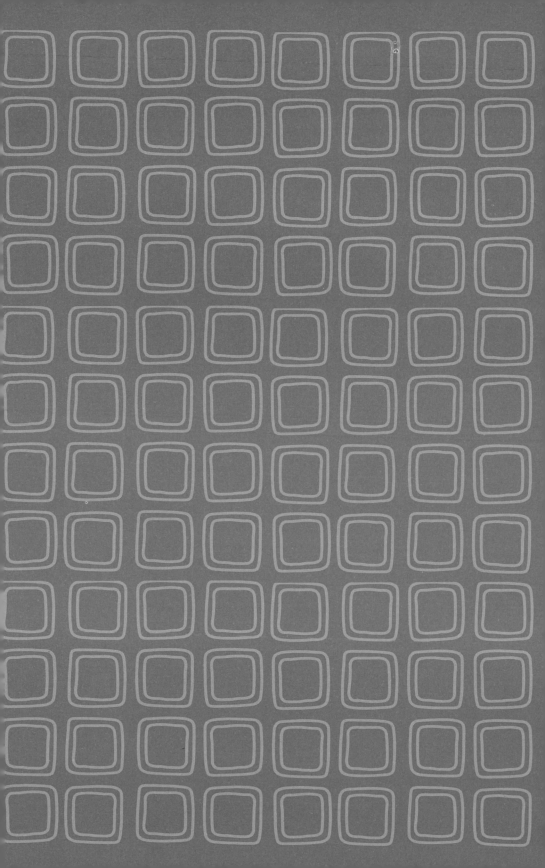

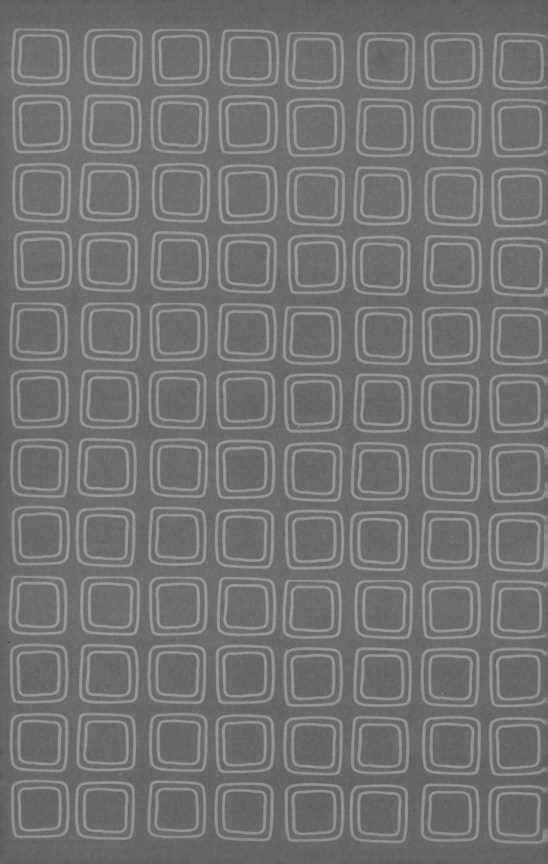